Medieval Mystery

PRAISE FOR *STORYSHARES*

"One of the brightest innovators and game-changers in the education industry."
– Forbes

"Your success in applying research-validated practices to promote literacy serves as a valuable model for other organizations seeking to create evidence-based literacy programs."
- Library of Congress

"We need powerful social and educational innovation, and Storyshares is breaking new ground. The organization addresses critical problems facing our students and teachers. I am excited about the strategies it brings to the collective work of making sure every student has an equal chance in life."
– Teach For America

"Around the world, this is one of the up-and-coming trailblazers changing the landscape of literacy and education."
- International Literacy Association

"It's the perfect idea. There's really nothing like this. I mean wow, this will be a wonderful experience for young people."   - Andrea Davis Pinkney, Executive Director, Scholastic

"Reading for meaning opens opportunities for a lifetime of learning. Providing emerging readers with engaging texts that are designed to offer both challenges and support for each individual will improve their lives for years to come. Storyshares is a wonderful start."
- David Rose, Co-founder of CAST & UDL

Medieval Mystery

Hanna Yeager

STORYSHARES

Story Share, Inc.
New York. Boston. Philadelphia

Published in the United States by Story Share, Inc.

Storyshares
Story Share, Inc.
24 N. Bryn Mawr Avenue #340
Bryn Mawr, PA 19010-3304
www.storyshares.org

Inspiring reading with a new kind of book.

Interest Level: Middle School
Grade Level Equivalent: 2.6

9781642611670

Book design by Storyshares

Printed in the United States of America

Storyshares Presents

1

Emmeline was not a coward, but right now she felt sick. Where had she seen his face before? She hadn't. But she had seen that same look on a man's face before. A hungry, greedy look.

He looked happy, in a mean way. Happy that he had found her out.

She told herself no one could have found out her secret. It had been four years since she had run away. Emmeline was now sixteen years old and free. Free from slavery.

Well, more or less.

The life of a serf in medieval England was not always easy. If a master was kind, life could be good. But if he was cruel, life would be miserable.

Some serfs were able to buy their freedom. Other serfs' masters wouldn't allow it. In those cases, there was only one thing to do: run away.

And for those runaway serfs, there was only one way to stay free: live in a town for a year and one day. Of course, this was hard to prove. Problems came when the courts wouldn't take a serf's word. They almost never did when an angry master was there.

If you were a runaway, it was better to avoid the courts altogether.

Emmeline smoothed her black hair as she hurried toward the kitchen. The sooner she got away from those prying eyes, the better.

The noise from the Great Hall faded away. The dark hallway was silent. Soon, the busy roar of the kitchen took its place.

Two huge fireplaces flamed against one wall. Many servants ran around the room. They stirred pots, chopped vegetables, and turned the roasting spits. It was very hot and noisy.

Emmeline did not want to stay any longer than she had to. She left her tray, moving back down the hallway to the buttery.

The buttery was downstairs, in the cellar. It was cool and quiet. Large barrels lined the walls of this room where the butler waited.

Emmeline handed him a pitcher. He filled it with wine from one of the barrels. The wine was dark red, like blood.

She turned to go and almost bumped into Mary.

Mary, the cooper's daughter, was a maid in Sir John's house. Her father made barrels in the village nearby. She was near Emmeline's age. Her freckled nose turned up at the tip. It made her look like an Irish elf, playful and full of tricks.

Mary liked to tell stories and make jokes about people. Sometimes she stretched the truth. But Emmeline liked her anyway. She couldn't help it. Mary always had a smile and a kind word.

Emmeline took a moment now to ask the question that was haunting her.

"Who is that old man?" she asked.

"What old man?" Mary asked.

"The one who serves Sir John," Emmeline said.

"Oh. Him," Mary said. "That's Richard Pratt. Or 'Prattler the Tattler' as he is known around here. He's Sir John's steward."

"I did not care for his look," Emmeline whispered.

"I know what you mean," Mary said. "His ugly old face is matched by a soul black as pitch."

Mary said it carelessly, without a thought. Emmeline was shocked by her boldness. She looked around quickly, but the butler didn't seem to have heard. Mary tossed her frizzy red curls and went on.

"Everybody says that Sir John rules with an iron fist. But we all know he owes his success to Pratt's tricks. Curse those eyes!" she said.

"You shouldn't say such things," Emmeline said.

"Why not? He's a spy and a traitor. Everyone knows it. Nobody likes him," Mary said.

"But surely—" Emmeline started to say.

"Don't worry about his feelings, lass," the butler cut in. "Pratt stopped caring what others thought of him before you were born."

That wasn't what Emmeline meant at all.

Aside from the fact that such talk could lead to trouble... it was gossip. No good ever came of speaking ill of another. Especially when they were not there.

But the butler and Mary continued to tell horrifying stories.

Pratt was a miser. He terrorized the peasants on Sir John's estate. He demanded much more of the farmers than he should. He had sold his childhood sweetheart to the Moors. He hated priests and the Church. He had traded his soul to the devil.

Each new story was wilder than the last.

Emmeline disliked the man. But she disliked gossip even more. It made an uneasy feeling in the pit of her stomach. She slipped out into the hallway.

Mary was right behind her with a final warning. "Keep your secrets close around that one," she said.

2

Red torches burned through the smoky haze. The Great Hall was full of people eating, drinking, and laughing. Minstrels played their instruments as loud as they could. Dogs rolled on the floor, barking and fighting over bones.

Here, as in the kitchen, there was a blazing fire. The room was almost warm. Bodyham Castle had never seen such a feast.

It wasn't every day that Sir John Dalyngrigge was to be married.

He sat behind the table at the end of the hall. He was a big, strong man of nearly thirty. He had a mane of honey-brown hair and a large nose. His booming laugh echoed in the hall. He was a lion of a man.

His bride-to-be was as unlike him as possible. Thin, pale, and timid. Lady Gwyneth trembled in the seat next to him at every loud noise. She was only twelve years old.

Emmeline felt sorry for her. Marriage at a young age was fairly common among English nobles. But that didn't make it any easier for the girls.

Gwyneth was not used to the rough jokes and horseplay of the men. It was her first time away from home. Her green eyes widened in fright as one man tackled another.

Over the floor they rolled, wrestling and grunting. They rolled into a group of fighting dogs. One of the men swore loudly when he was bitten.

Sir John roared with laughter.

Gwyneth looked as if she would faint.

Emmeline hurried to her side. "Here is your wine, my lady," she said.

Gwyneth leaned back and whispered, "I don't know how long I can bear this!"

She was a sensitive girl, and nervous. Emmeline looked around for Gwyneth's parents. They were nowhere in sight. To leave their own child in a place such as this!

But then, they had arranged the marriage because of the fame it would bring. Not for their daughter's comfort.

"Drink this, my lady," Emmeline said.

Her mistress seized the cup and swallowed a mouthful. She looked at Emmeline with pleading eyes.

"Oh, for a bit of peace!" Gwyneth said. "If only you could play something. Sing something. It would make me feel better."

Emmeline did not see how such a thing could be done. In the privacy of her lady's apartments was one thing, but this...

She looked at the sea of faces around her and felt dizzy. There was no one to turn to for help.

A young man caught her gaze. He was waving to her. Hardly aware of what she was doing, Emmeline moved in his direction.

"Hullo! My man seems to have gone missing in his search for ale. Would you mind giving me some of yours?" the man asked.

Emmeline moved to obey. Her mind was on other things.

Then the man winked at her boldly. "You have such beautiful eyes. A pity you won't raise them from the tabletop," he said.

Emmeline flushed and nearly spilled the wine.

When he took the goblet, their hands met. For an instant, their eyes met, too.

His were blue as the summer sky and sparkling with laughter. His tone was meant to be soft, yet the voice was raspy. A military man, used to giving orders. Taking a long drink from the cup, he smacked his lips.

"Well, it's not ale, but it'll do nicely!" he said.

Emmeline backed away quickly as he smiled. She took her place behind her lady. She did not look in the knight's direction again.

Sir John banged his drinking horn on the table for silence. When a hush had fallen, he leaned toward Gwyneth.

"Well, my dear. It is your turn to choose the entertainment. What shall it be? A dance, story, or special tune?" he asked.

Gwyneth shook her head shyly.

"Come, come! Perhaps one of these wretches will tumble for your enjoyment," Sir John said.

He leaned closer to whisper, "Surely you would not rob me of a chance to please you."

A blush crept into Gwyneth's cheek. Quietly, she stammered her request.

Sir John rose to face the assembly.

"It seems that my love favors sweet song above all," he said. "She asks that her maid be allowed to delight us."

He smiled boldly at Emmeline, who felt herself grow pale.

Oh, no. It was the worst possible time! And in front of all these ale-soaked ruffians. But a servant must obey.

Emmeline left the table and went to the minstrels. She asked one of them for the loan of his harp. He handed it to her with a wide grin.

His smile asked, *What would this girl do?*

His rudeness stirred her blood. In a flash of anger, she forgot about fear.

In the silence of the hall, the blood sang in her ears. Pounding and rushing like the sea. She closed her eyes.

No. Not the sea.

Her fingers plucked the strings. They were feeling for a sound in her memory. It was a rushing, flowing sound. The sound a stream makes on the first day of spring.

She plucked the strings lightly. Bouncing along pebbles until she reached deeper water. Long, flowing patterns, like ripples in the stream.

Then the words came. Slowly, at first. Strange words in a strange language.

Her lips formed them. Still, Emmeline did not know where they came from. They were soft, and sometimes deep. Grass pushed up from underneath the snow.

It was about spring, this song. Spring in a far-off country. There were small birds in the trees. Strange, yet also familiar. A door began to open in her memory.

But the song came to an end. She opened her eyes, blinking back tears of disappointment.

The hall erupted with applause. Sir John pounded his hands together. The young knight beamed with pleasure. Gwyneth's face showed an odd expression. Behind Gwyneth and Sir John was the triumphant face of Richard Pratt.

Emmeline turned from his hungry look and escaped the room.

3

Tap. Tap. Tap.

It came again. That quiet knocking. It would not be ignored.

Emmeline was exhausted. She had gotten her young mistress safely away from the Great Hall. But then she had to calm Gwyneth down so she could sleep.

That had been an hour ago. It was past midnight, now. But whoever was outside the door would not leave.

Finally, she got up, pulling on a cloak.

The glow from the fireplace did not show her visitor at once. When he did show his face, Emmeline stepped back quickly.

It was Richard Pratt.

He closed the door softly. Then he looked around the room carefully.

"Can I help you?" Emmeline forced herself to speak.

He smiled. Or at least, he tried to smile. It twisted his face in a horrible way. Much more frightening now than in the Great Hall.

Emmeline retreated another step.

"Aye, that you can, lass," Pratt said. His voice was smooth as oil. She shuddered as his eyes glittered. "My master would like a word with you. If it is not... too much trouble."

His choice of words was cruel. He was a free man. Emmeline was a bondwoman. She had to do what she was told, or suffer for it. But she was Gwyneth's maid, not Sir John's servant.

She glanced at her mistress's door. What if she woke Gwyneth?

"No, lass," he said. "I wouldn't try it."

"Who do you think you are, ordering me about?" she asked.

Pratt showed his teeth. "Once upon a time there was a pretty girl," he said. "A man fell in love with her. But she ran away."

A chill washed over Emmeline.

He knew. In spite of everything she had done to hide it.

He fixed her with a cold stare.

"The man was her old master. And he is still looking for her," he said. "Devonshire is far away. But not far enough. Come along now, like a good girl."

What else could she do? Maybe if she went with him, he would keep her secret.

Heaving a sigh, she followed him into the hallway. Silently, they passed from the household apartments to the chapel. A candle flickered in the darkness near the altar.

Emmeline crossed herself. She whispered a prayer as she walked.

They seemed to be walking forever. When they passed windows, she could hear rain falling.

They moved through two black, echoing chambers. An odd, mocking echo seemed to chase after Emmeline's footsteps. She felt that she was being watched. But when she turned to look, there was nothing.

Finally, they entered a smaller room. A large chair sat in front of the fire.

"Good evening, master," Pratt said.

"Pratt? Is that you?" Sir John's voice sounded lazy.

Emmeline planted her feet stubbornly when Pratt grabbed her arm. But he still yanked her toward the fireplace.

Sir John lounged in the chair, one leg thrown over the arm. He held a cup in one hand. He grinned when he saw Emmeline.

"Oh, so you've come after all, have you?" he asked.

"Yes, my lord," Emmeline said.

Her tone was flat. She kept her eyes fixed firmly on the floor.

He leaned forward, looking up into her face. He was trying to make her look at him. But she wouldn't give him the satisfaction.

He waved a hand, dismissing his steward. As Pratt left, Sir John spoke again.

"What is your name?" he asked.

"Emmeline, my lord," she said.

"Emmeline! How enchanting," he said. "It means 'little rival.' Did you know that?"

"No, my lord," she said.

He laughed softly. "You are trying to be difficult, aren't you?" he asked.

The girl was silent.

The man shifted impatiently, waving his hand toward the corner. "Play for me," he said.

Emmeline turned to follow his hand.

A small harp, beautifully made, rested on a bench. She took it in her hands and sat down. She thought of David, calming the restless spirit of his king. She brushed the strings softly.

"No, no. Not like that," Sir John said. He sipped the wine. "Play the way you did in the hall."

She stopped.

He spoke again. "Come here. Here. Sit on the rug at my feet."

Up until this point, Emmeline had been uneasy. Now, she became suspicious. But she got up and went to the man's chair.

Kneeling down, she pulled her cloak more tightly about her shoulders. Her nightdress underneath felt thin and flimsy. She kept as far away from Sir John as she could manage.

"You needn't be afraid of me, girl. I won't bite," he said.

She ignored him and began to play again.

"Sing," Sir John said.

Emmeline did not feel like singing. She was becoming angry with Sir John's demands. The harp was silent. She glared up at the man fiercely.

He chuckled deep in his throat.

"What an enchanting creature you are!" he said. "If looks could kill... what a charming murderess you would make."

Her face flushed with shame and confusion. Emmeline jumped to her feet and turned to run.

But Sir John also got up. His strong hand gripped her arm. His hand was hard as iron. His voice was suddenly soft and pleading.

"Don't go. Please, don't leave," he said. "I... need you, Emmeline."

His breath brushed her hair. She could smell wine. He had had more than his fair share for the night.

Wine had made him bold. And Emmeline was afraid. But fear did not rob her of common sense. She must act carefully, now.

"My lord," she said. She turned to face him slowly. "Soon you will be married. Your wife will be your comfort."

"Gwyneth is terrified of me. She lacks your spirit," he said.

"Whose fault is that?" she asked.

"Well, I—" he stammered. "I do not have the pleasing ways of a minstrel! To charm my way to a lady's heart. I am a rough soldier. With no time to recite poetry or such nonsense."

Emmeline gently freed her arm from his grasp. "Perhaps your attempt to learn such 'nonsense' will win your lady's heart," she said.

She turned to go, but his voice stopped her at the door.

"Please accept my gift," he said. "The harp is yours."

It was tempting. Emmeline looked longingly at its carved shape. She could never hope to own an instrument half so fine. But she shook her head.

"I am sorry, my lord," she said. "But I cannot accept such a gift."

She slipped out into the passage before she could see his disappointment.

4

"I can't wait until I'm free of them," Gwyneth said.

"Free of whom, my lady?" Emmeline asked.

"Who else? My parents," Gwyneth said. She frowned at the path she walked.

Emmeline was just a step behind her. The path led across the courtyard of Bodyham Castle.

Gwyneth's parents had always given their daughter everything she wanted. But, like most spoiled children, it was never enough.

Emmeline sighed on the inside. Out loud, she said, "Tomorrow is your wedding day, my lady—"

"Don't 'my lady' me, Emmy!" Gwyneth interrupted. "Oh. I see I've upset you."

Emmeline was upset, but she was trying to hide it. It was not Gwyneth's fault. She simply could not forget the events of last night.

It all seemed like a nightmare. Pratt had discovered her secret. Now he held it like a club over her head. If she wasn't careful, he would let it fall.

And then there was Sir John. He had nearly declared that he loved her, a servant! It was unthinkable. And yet, it had happened. Another secret she could not reveal to anyone.

But perhaps she could talk to the priest, Father Alban. With that thought, Emmeline felt better.

Gwyneth sighed. She looked at the stone walls.

"I feel trapped in here, Emmy. Let's go up and have a look around," she said.

Soon, the two girls found themselves on top of the outer wall. The view was wonderful.

The world was newly washed by last night's rain. Not a ripple disturbed the water in the castle's moat. Slim trees stood by the water's edge. Their branches held a mist of new, green leaves.

"Do you remember when I found you?" Gwyneth asked with pride.

"Of course, my—" Emmeline started to say.

"Oh, please stop, dear. Call me Gwenny, the way you used to," Gwyneth said.

Gwyneth looped her arm through Emmeline's. She leaned her head on the older girl's shoulder. Gwyneth had always been an affectionate child.

Gwyneth's long blonde hair was bright as a canary's wing. Like a canary, her movements were quick and birdlike. She looked at Emmeline from the corner of her eye. Waiting for her answer.

They walked in silence for a time before the dark-haired girl spoke.

"Of course I remember," Emmeline said. "How could I ever forget? I was miserable and hungry. Even before the weaver turned me out."

"I was so angry when I heard about that! How could that awful old woman turn you away?" Gwyneth asked. She pressed Emmeline's arm protectively. "You wove the best linen I'd ever seen before or since!"

Emmeline felt a little glow inside.

"You won't ever leave me, will you?" Gwyneth asked. Her voice was full of a sudden fear.

Emmeline bit her lip. She tried to find the right words.

"Gwenny, dear. Tomorrow you will be married," she said.

"So everyone keeps telling me," Gwyneth said.

The servant took her mistress's hand. "Marriage is a holy state. I will always be your friend," she said, smiling. "But between a husband and wife there is a special bond. No friendship can equal it."

"But, but—" Gwyneth stammered. "You won't ever go off and get married, will you?"

Emmeline took a moment to think before answering. "I cannot see such a thing in my future," she said.

"Well, I can!" Gwyneth giggled. "Emmy, you should have seen all those men's faces last night! After you sang, I mean. Every one of them was madly in love with you!"

Emmeline blinked. She could never get used to Gwyneth's sudden changes of mood. Even after nearly four years.

All she could find to say was, "I hope not!"

"I did it on purpose, you know," Gwyneth said.

"Did what on purpose?" Emmeline asked.

Gwyneth grinned. Her green eyes sparkled. She looked like a naughty fairy.

"I wanted you to sing because it would make a good impression," she said. "Don't look at me like that! I can't sing worth beans. We all know that singing is a proper lady's talent. If I can't sing well, at least I have a maid who can!"

There was no sting in what she said. Somehow, Gwyneth could make a person almost like being used. She was just that charming.

Gwyneth began pushing Emmeline along. She steered her toward the northwest tower. She continued to talk excitedly.

"Now that I'll have a handsome husband, I want the same for you," she said. "Pick one. Pick any one of these fine men here and I'll—"

Emmeline was laughing now. "Shhh, Gwenny! They might hear you!"

"I hope they do! Hear ye, hear ye," Gwyneth began in a loud voice.

Some of the servants down below looked up curiously. Gwyneth was pleased by the attention. She went on.

"I am on a quest for my friend, the noble Emmeline," she said, pointing to her embarrassed maid. "Who has made known her great desire to find a handsome—"

Gwyneth looked at Emmeline. But Emmeline was no longer there. She was running toward the tower to escape from all the attention.

Gwyneth hitched up her skirts in a most unladylike way. Then she ran off after Emmeline.

When she caught up with Emmeline, she found her laughing helplessly.

Emmeline leaned against the tower wall and gasped, "Oh, Gwenny! How could you? They will all think we're mad!"

Emmeline fought to control herself.

Gwyneth made a solemn pose. Kneeling at Emmeline's feet and folding her hands, she whispered, "Suitor, say unto me thy suit."

They both collapsed into giggles.

"Have they gone?" Emmeline asked.

She looked out to see if the crowd of servants had gone. Some of them were still standing around.

Turning, she dashed to the tower stairs...

Straight into the arms of the bold young knight.

5

Sir Hugh was surprised. The very girl he had been thinking about. And she had just thrown herself into his arms!

His arms closed around her. She had the deepest blue eyes he had ever seen. They stared up at him as she struggled to get free.

He took a step back. The edge of the stairway dropped off under his heel.

Hugh staggered. The girl grabbed him, saving him from a fall.

For a moment they balanced on the edge. His own steely blue eyes fastened on the maid's. They breathed together in the silence.

"Where are you going in such a hurry, my lady?" he asked.

With his words, the spell was broken. She pulled away.

Hugh had never been in danger of falling down the stairs. He had only used it to get close to the girl. She was beautiful and shy. Like a wild deer. Ready to leap away at the smallest sign of danger.

"I was... Well, I was going to, um—" Emmeline stammered.

"She was going to show me the prison, Sir Knight," Gwyneth said quickly. "We wanted to see the guard rooms and everything! You will show us, won't you?"

"Certainly, my lady," he said, bowing. "But first, I must insist that you call me by my name. Sir Hugh, at your service."

He couldn't have been more pleased. It was the chance he'd been praying for.

"I'm Gwyneth. That is, Lady Gwyneth," she said. "This is my... friend, Emmeline."

"It will be my pleasure to take you both wherever you wish. But the dungeon... surely you would not wish to go there," he said, in a deeper tone. "Nasty, dark, and damp. A miserable hole for miserable wretches."

"Well, Sir Hugh. Soon, I will be mistress of this place. It only seems right that I should know about everything. Wouldn't you agree?" Gwyneth asked.

Hugh was amused. Gwyneth seemed to have gotten over her nervousness of last night. Was it because there were just the three of them? Or did her silent friend's company give her courage?

"Spoken like a commander, my lady. One must know the field of battle, eh?" he asked, grinning.

The girl named Emmeline blushed.

For the rest of the afternoon, they explored the castle. Everything from the dungeon to the dovecote.

Gwyneth seemed to enjoy the dovecote more than the dungeon. Listening to the doves cooing in their nesting boxes was more pleasant.

Through it all, Sir Hugh made an excellent guide.

He had the feeling that Lady Gwyneth was trying to play matchmaker. A game which, in this case, he fully supported.

But Emmeline was having none of it.

That she liked Sir Hugh was clear, even to him. But she was very reserved and quiet. Maybe she was trying to make up for the morning's embarrassment. But once, he was surprised to see a look of fear in her eyes. Turning, he saw Sir John pass by a doorway.

At age twenty-two, Hugh was the captain of the household guard. He had been a military man since he was fourteen, but he had some skill when it came to solving mysteries. Or at least, he liked to think that he did.

Why would Emmeline be afraid of Sir John?

Hugh thought it over and couldn't come up with a reason. Sir John was loud sometimes, but his bark was worse than his bite. He drank too much at times. But then, so did most men.

Sir John was tall and handsome, if Hugh was any judge. But why would anyone be afraid of a man because of that?

After they had explored the castle, Hugh took them across the moat. Emmeline seemed to breathe easier among the trees. She looked at home on the green grass. The wind played with her long, black hair. She was picking wildflowers at the water's edge.

Lady Gwyneth asked Hugh a question. He turned his attention to her. When he looked for Emmeline again, he couldn't see her.

He stood and moved closer to the water. She must have gone in among the willows.

He heard the sound of voices. Hugh couldn't make out the words. But he could hear a man's voice. It was harsh and demanding. Then there was silence.

A moment later, Richard Pratt came out from the trees. He walked to the bridge and crossed the moat.

"Now, what was that all about?" Hugh muttered to himself.

He returned to his seat near Lady Gwyneth. Or, at least, where Gwyneth had been sitting. She was nowhere in sight.

It took a little time to find both ladies. And they both seemed to be out of sorts. Emmeline tried to be cheerful for her mistress. But a sadness seemed to hang about her.

Gwyneth said she was "tired out of her wits." And anyway, it was time for the evening meal. Another feast was in the making.

These days, life was short and often brutal. It was good to make a celebration last as long as possible.

6

Sir John paced back and forth impatiently. Like a lion in its cage.

When would she come? She should have been there an hour ago.

He leaned over and stared at his shadow in the water. He had decided to meet Emmeline at the castle well, in the basement of the tower. The basement was connected to the kitchen. It was deserted at this late hour. After all, no sense in being seen.

Sir John didn't know what kind of spell she had cast. He could think of nothing but Emmeline. Her eyes, her grace, the sound of her voice.

It was the night before his wedding. And he was madly in love with his fiancée's maid.

Emmeline did not love him back. Not yet.

Sir John was not used to being rejected by any woman. Certainly not by a servant.

She would learn her place. Hadn't his father, Sir Edward, crushed the peasant revolt of 1381? The same blood flowed in Sir John's veins. He would show her that he was not to be toyed with.

It had to be nearly three in the morning. The "witching hour," as some called it. His head still buzzed faintly from the ale he'd drunk at supper.

A slight scuffling sounded from the top of the stairs. Pratt was up there, acting as a lookout.

Sir John looked up when he heard a woman's voice. It spoke in a low, but passionate, tone.

Suddenly, there was a wild cry.

Richard Pratt screamed as he fell headfirst down the steps. His body twisted horribly. His head hit the bottom step with a sickening crack.

For a moment, Sir John stood in shock.

Blood dripped and pooled on the stone floor beneath Pratt's head. He didn't move. He didn't seem to be breathing, either.

"Captain of the guard!" Sir John roared, racing up the stairs.

He ran into a sleepy-eyed cook. Sir John grabbed him by the front of his tunic.

"Fetch Sir Hugh immediately! Do you hear? There's been a murder!"

7

Emmeline stood frozen in the kitchen doorway. The cup she held clattered to the floor.

Sir John spun to face her. "You!" he cried. "I never would have thought!"

He crossed the room in a few strides and grabbed her arm. He looked down at her curiously.

"But, then again... why not?" he asked.

Sir Hugh ran into the room. He was still buckling on his swordbelt.

"What happened?" he asked. He looked from Sir John to Emmeline, then back again.

"Murder, Captain. And I have the murderer right here," Sir John said. He dragged Emmeline forward.

A pained look crossed Hugh's face. All he said was, "We will see if that is so. Where is the body?"

"At the bottom of the stairs," Sir John said.

The captain disappeared down the stairs.

The cook had returned. He looked less sleepy and more nervous. He kept darting looks toward Emmeline.

A few servants looked curiously into the kitchen doorway. They disappeared when Sir John glared at them.

Hugh came up the stairs. He turned to the cook. "Fetch William Barber at once!" he said. "That man is not dead. He seems to have cracked his skull. He must have been pushed quite hard."

"That is exactly what happened, Captain," Sir John said. "I heard a woman's voice from the top of the stairs. Then Pratt screamed. I thought he was dead, the way he landed. I raced upstairs in time to catch the criminal."

"I see," Hugh said. He turned to Emmeline. "And what were you doing here?"

Sir John was impatient. "I've already told you, Captain, she—" he started to say.

"I heard what you said, my lord. But I'd like to hear it from her, if you don't mind," Hugh said.

Emmeline opened her mouth. But no sound came out. She tried again.

"I was... that is, I... I came for a cup of water," she said.

"A likely story!" Sir John said.

It did sound weak. But Hugh was becoming impatient with Sir John's accusations.

"My lord," he said. "Would you mind telling me what you were doing? Down by the well. At three in the morning."

"Well, I was... I don't see what that has to do with anything!" Sir John said.

"It might have a great deal to do with it," Hugh said.

Sir John looked ready to explode.

Just then the barber entered, followed by the cook. The barber's duties were not limited to cutting hair. He was also a doctor, if there was need.

He came down the tower stairs. The cook whispered something into Hugh's ear. Sir Hugh looked very serious.

"I'm sorry, miss," he said. "But I'm afraid I must place you under arrest."

Emmeline was terrified. She felt hopeless and desperate. The fear coursing through her body gave her a surge of strength.

Yanking her arm from Sir John's grip, she ran. Out the kitchen door. Down the dark passage. Through the Great Hall and up the spiral staircase. Through the room where she had met Sir John the night before.

She could hear the shouts and pounding feet.

They were gaining on her. Catching up a stool, she threw it backwards. A yell told her that she had found a target.

She ran down the long hall and through the smaller room beyond. Her breath came in gasps. She was racing to the one place where she would be safe.

Throwing open the chapel door, she jerked to a stop. Someone had grabbed the sleeve of her dress. With a sound of shredding fabric, she pulled herself through the door.

Sanctuary.

8

"Well, this is just splendid," Hugh said.

He leaned back in the chair and rubbed his eyes. He hadn't gotten more than two hours of sleep. His mind did not want to work. He either knew too much or not enough to solve this mystery.

He had given orders that no one was to leave the castle. Not until he arrested whoever had tried to kill Richard Pratt.

Twelve hours of questioning servants and guests. Twelve hours of frustration! Everyone knew something, but no one was guilty. Or at least everyone had an excuse.

Sir John had seemed tense and angry. "Are you mad? Why would I kill my own steward? I'll admit I had no love for the man. But he was loyal. He did his duty," he said.

Hugh had challenged him. "Isn't it true that you were heard arguing with him yesterday? Arguing quite angrily?" he asked. "Just what were you doing in the southwest tower last night? Perhaps you killed him and blamed another."

Well, that was a tricky situation. Sir Hugh worked for Sir John, after all. He could only push the man so far. Whatever Sir John had been doing by the well would stay his secret. There was no getting it out of him.

John Cook had seen Emmeline in the kitchen when he arrived. Mere seconds after the bloodcurdling scream. John Cook lived on the second floor of the tower. The better to keep an eye on kitchen business. He had no love for Richard Pratt, either.

James Butler had some strange tales to tell about Pratt. James disliked Pratt because he was a greedy miser who never drank.

"Always too fond of gold and such like," he said. "And I never did trust a man who wouldn't drink."

Then there were the common soldiers, serving maids, and footmen. All of them had rumors to whisper of the near-departed. But most of them had sound excuses for themselves.

One of the stable boys had been known to mutter threats. He was nearly hot-headed enough to follow through. But then, it had been a woman's voice at the stairs.

Catherine, the scullery maid, had a hot temper. Almost as scalding as her dishwater. She had never forgiven Pratt for sending her sweetheart away years before.

Pratt had found out about Catherine's romance with a shepherd boy. Pratt had sent the boy to one of Sir John's distant estates. To this day, he tended sheep on the lonely hillsides far away. Hatred boiled over in Catherine's eyes at the mention of Pratt.

But she had been staying with her sick mother in the village. She had only returned to the castle a few hours ago. She couldn't have had a hand in last night's trouble.

"What is that you say, sir?" a young man with a mop of curly brown hair asked.

"Oh, nothing, Andrew," Hugh said. He let his chair down with a bang. "Pratt seems to have been quite a terrible fellow. At first I wondered who tried to murder him. Now I'm beginning to wonder if there is anyone who didn't want to."

Hugh's squire laughed. "I know what you mean, sir. My Mary, she has some stories that would make your hair curl!" Andrew said.

"No, thank you, Andrew. I've had more than enough of those," Hugh said.

They sat in silence for a few moments. Hugh chewed on the tip of his thumb. The younger man oiled his master's saddle. Then Andrew stopped working. He had an odd look on his face.

"You know, I think there is one," he said.

"One what?" Hugh asked.

"One person who didn't hate Old Pratt," Andrew said. His forehead wrinkled in thought. "My Mary, she said that lady's maid, Emmeline, spoke up for him."

"What?" Hugh asked, surprised.

"Yes, sir," Andrew said. "Mary and James Butler were telling stories, the way they do. And Emmeline, she disagreed. Left the room, in fact."

Well, that was something. It was unlikely that someone would defend a person's name one day only to murder them the next.

It was the first hopeful bit of news he'd heard all day. Hugh stood and stepped to the guard room door.

"If anyone needs me, Andrew, tell them I'm at prayers," he said.

9

"There is no need to be afraid. I will not try to drag you out again. Besides," Hugh said, grinning, "you're quite handy with a stool."

"I am sorry about that," Emmeline said.

"Don't be. I'll recover. Which is more than I can say for your old friend," Hugh said.

Emmeline stiffened at his last words. Hugh noticed her quick breath.

"How is he?" she asked.

She sounded and looked as if she really cared. It was unlikely that a killer could fake such concern. Still...

"Not very well, I'm afraid. I think he will not wake again," Hugh said. "The surgeon is supposed to drill a hole in his skull today. He says it will let the bad blood out. But they'd have to drain every drop from his body to do that."

The girl was silent. She sat on the end of the bench opposite Hugh. Her sleeve was torn from the shoulder where he'd grabbed it. She looked cold. Cold and sad.

Hugh tried to forget that he was falling in love with her. He told himself that she had tried to murder a man. But he couldn't make himself believe it. His next words were spoken softly.

"How did he threaten to hurt you?" he asked.

Emmeline was surprised. Her blue eyes widened, then narrowed.

"If I tell you, will you swear not to send me back?" she asked.

"Back where?" Hugh asked.

"Devonshire," she said.

"What's in Devonshire?" he asked.

Emmeline swallowed. "My old master," she said.

Suddenly, Hugh understood. Here was a reason for murder if he ever saw one. And yet, she had trusted him with this information.

She knew what it might mean. If Richard Pratt died, she would be thought guilty. Unless Hugh could prove otherwise.

The penalty Emmeline faced was harsh. If a woman was convicted of murder, she would be strangled, then burned.

Hugh decided to risk an unusual question.

"Do you know why Sir John was at the well last night?" he asked.

"Yes," Emmeline said.

"Tell me," he said.

"I— I would rather not," she said.

"Why not?" he asked.

"Because— Oh, Hugh, I'm so ashamed!" Emmeline cried.

He was surprised by her sudden tears. Without thinking, he reached out to comfort her. For a few moments he held her against his shoulder.

The priest, Father Alban, looked out from the sacristy. Seeing that all was well, he disappeared from sight.

The sanctuary lamp glowed with a warm, red light. It flickered on floor tiles of yellow and green. A shaft of sunlight lit up the sky outside the window. And somewhere, a bird sang.

"Two nights ago, Richard Pratt came to my room," Emmeline said. "He told me that Sir John wished to speak with me. I didn't want to go. Gwyneth was asleep... and I was frightened."

"But you went?" Hugh asked.

"Yes," she said.

What Emmeline didn't know was that she had been seen. Sometimes, it seemed like the walls really did have ears. And eyes. News traveled fast in a small place.

"What did Sir John say?" Hugh asked.

"At first, he made fun of me," Emmeline said. "I tried to leave, but he stopped me. He told me that he needed me. I was afraid. He is a very strong man."

Hugh could feel himself getting angry. How could the man act like such a beast? And only a few days before his wedding, too!

Emmeline went on. "I didn't listen to him. And I didn't stay. He tried to give me a gift. But I would not accept it," she said.

Her words explained so much. Now Hugh knew why Sir John was so quick to accuse her. His pride was hurt. He had been rejected by a servant. But one question still had not been answered.

"You haven't told me why he was by the well last night," he said.

"Oh," Emmeline said. She sat up straight. "Yesterday, when we were outside, Richard Pratt spoke to me. Sir John ordered me to meet him at the well at two o'clock."

"But you didn't come until three," Hugh said.

"I didn't want to go at all!" Emmeline said. "I had decided to disobey Sir John. I was terrified of what might happen. But I was glad, too."

She sighed. "Then Lady Gwyneth needed a drink of water. I wasted as much time as possible before I finally went. I didn't want to meet Sir John or Richard Pratt," she said.

"But you went, after all," Hugh said. He was thoughtful. "At a time when no one expected you."

But it hadn't been unexpected to one person.

10

Mary could hardly contain herself. The news was too good to keep. And straight from the source, too! Andrew always told her everything.

Quickly, she folded the sheets. Crossing the courtyard, she walked to the guest rooms. Mary knocked on a bedroom door.

"Come in," a voice called.

When she entered, she saw Rachel. Rachel was the Lady Gwyneth's old nursemaid. And a good friend of Mary's.

Rachel was sitting by the fire, spinning wool into yarn. Her fingers were quick and steady. They pulled the fluffy sheep's wool into strong thread.

Mary turned to the bed and began to remake it. It seemed to take forever. And she couldn't wait to tell Rachel what she knew! Impatiently, she smoothed the blankets and beat the pillows.

"Have you heard any news?" Rachel finally asked.

"Oh... A little something," Mary said. She tried to sound like it wasn't worth repeating.

"Well, girl, out with it!" Rachel said.

"I was talking to Andrew this afternoon. About the murder and all. Well, he said that William Barber said... Richard Pratt will live to tell us all who his murderer is!" Mary dropped the words impressively.

And Rachel was impressed. She set her wooden spindle in her lap.

"Well, Mary, I've always said that wonders never end," she said. "To think I'd live to see the day when a dead man would accuse his own murderer!"

Forgotten was the fact that Pratt had never actually died. It was so unnatural not to die when one was "murdered." And as for having holes drilled in one's head...

Old Rachel shook her head. Doctors these days thought they were smarter than anyone. Even God Himself.

Rachel stated her opinion as strongly as she always did.

"We should let the Lord decide life and death. Not some man who thinks he can make the dead speak!" she said.

11

It was the witching hour once again.

A shadow moved through the guest rooms. Silently gliding past sleeping forms.

It reached the chapel door and passed through.

There was a girl sleeping on a bench near the altar. The shadow stopped for a moment, looking down. Then it passed through the opposite door into the room beyond.

There was a guard posted outside the door to the East Tower. Sir Hugh's squire was protecting the witness. The shadow hung back, waiting.

Andrew yawned and shook his head. He stretched his neck and looked to the right and left.

Nothing.

He leaned back against the door. His eyes blinked sleepily. Finally, they closed.

The shadow moved forward slowly. It did not go to the door. It stood in front of the fireplace beside the door.

The fire had long since died. But a few coals still glowed. The hearthstone was warm.

Then, the shadow seemed suddenly to plunge into the chimney stones!

At the end of the fireplace passage was the East Tower room. On a bed in the corner lay the old man.

A little moonlight came in through a narrow window. It made a white puddle on the floor. The shadow seemed hesitant to step through it. Finally, it did so.

The old man was asleep. He did not move. His breath whistled out through his lips.

The shadow reached into the folds of its cloak. It pulled out a small bottle. Uncorking it, the shadow held it above the old man's mouth.

"Stop where you are!" a voice called.

The heavy door banged open, flooding the room with torchlight. The cloaked shadow tried to escape through the secret passage. But the passage was blocked by Sir Hugh. Catching it around the body, he tore the hood from its head.

Long, golden hair spilled down like a waterfall. Angry green eyes glared in the light.

It was Lady Gwyneth.

"Well, my lady. Have you come to visit the sick?" Hugh asked.

She struggled, but Hugh wrestled the bottle from her hand. Taking a sniff, he frowned and threw it in the corner. The sound of shattering glass was loud in the sudden silence.

"Belladonna. A deadly poison," Hugh said. "Perhaps you were trying to give him eternal rest? The man you already tried to kill once? Answer me!"

Hugh gave the girl a shake.

When she spoke, it was in an ugly tone. "You know nothing!" Gwyneth said. "Let me go! Sir John will not stand for this."

Sir John's voice came from outside the room. It sounded tired and defeated.

"Lock her up, Hugh," he said.

12

"My lady, please—" Emmeline said.

"I don't want to hear it! I don't want your pity. I hate you!" Gwyneth screamed and beat her fists on the iron bars.

Her hands were bruised, but she didn't seem to feel anything. Except hate.

"This is all your fault!" she raged. "First, you stole Sir John. Then you lied to me! I never want to see you again!"

She broke down sobbing and slid to the floor. She began muttering to herself. Twisting her hair around her fingers. She looked at her dress. Her hand touched the red fabric lovingly.

"Pretty. Pretty color," she murmured.

Red had always been Gwyneth's favorite color.

Emmeline choked back her own tears. She turned away, falling to her knees. How could God allow such a thing to happen? Gwyneth was completely mad. This girl that Emmeline loved now hated her with all her might.

"I'm sorry. I'm so sorry, Gwenny. I could never be what you needed," Emmeline said.

She looked back. Their eyes met. Gwyneth's were like hard, green marbles. Empty and resentful.

Emmeline stumbled to her feet and up the stairs. Maybe she shouldn't have come.

Slowly, she walked through the servants' rooms and out into the courtyard. She walked through the gatehouse.

She didn't know where she was going. Her broken heart pushed her onward. She crossed the moat and came to the end of the bridge.

Emmeline sank to the ground underneath an oak tree. She sat there for a very long time.

"Are you all right, my child?" It was Father Alban's voice.

No. She would never be all right again.

The old priest sat down, resting his back against the oak.

"You know, gossip is a terrible sin," he said.

"Yes, Father," Emmeline said.

"It is a lot like murder," he said. "Only, instead of killing our neighbor, we kill his good name."

Emmeline thought about that. He was right, of course. In this case, gossip had nearly caused a real death. But she still felt that she was to blame.

"Father... Is it a sin to keep a secret?" she asked.

"What kind of secret?" Father Alban asked.

Emmeline's hands twisted together.

"I felt so ashamed by Sir John's behavior. I didn't want anyone to know," she said. "I felt like it was my fault, somehow. Oh! If only I had talked to you before all this happened!"

"My child," Father Alban said. "The seed of jealousy was planted in Gwyneth's heart long ago. It is a common thing. Sad, but common. She was unhappy with herself, so she tried to blame you."

"Will she ever be well again?" Emmeline asked. She was begging for some hope.

"Perhaps. But that will be up to her. You have done your best. Let God take care of her now," he said.

Emmeline thought about everything that had happened in the last few days. Hugh had told her the whole story. The night Emmeline had talked to Sir John, she had been seen. By Mary Cooper.

Mary had a nose for trouble and scandal. She had followed Pratt and Emmeline, to see where they went. Mary was also friendly with Rachel, Gwyneth's nursemaid.

Mary told Rachel about what she had seen. Rachel then mentioned it to Gwyneth's mother. Gwyneth overheard everything.

Gwyneth was extremely jealous by nature. She never thought that Emmeline might dislike Sir John. In her mind, Emmeline had become her rival.

Gwyneth was angry, but willing to give her maid a second chance. She had even tried to interest her in another man. Then she overheard Pratt talking to Emmeline outside the castle.

In a fit of jealous rage, the girl had planned to hurt Emmeline.

Later that night, Gwyneth emptied the water from the pitcher in her room. Then she told Emmeline to fetch a cup of water from the well.

While Emmeline finished some small chores, Gwyneth crept into the kitchen. She planned to arrive before her maid. So she was surprised to find that Emmeline had arrived before her.

Or so she thought.

In the dim light, she mistook Richard Pratt for Emmeline. They were about the same height. With bitter words she ran at him, knocking him down the stairs.

Of course, as soon as he screamed, she realized her mistake. In a panic, she fled the kitchen. Emmeline arrived just in time to be seen by the cook.

The rest of the story was quickly told. Gwyneth made full use of her mistake. She was quite happy to have the blame fall on Emmeline. But then she heard the rumor that Richard Pratt was going to talk.

The rumor had been started by Sir Hugh. With it, he hoped to expose the killer.

Gwyneth didn't know if Pratt had recognized her. But her guilty mind didn't want to take a chance. She was afraid that if Pratt talked, he would accuse her. She couldn't stand the thought of going to prison.

So she had crept into the East Tower using a secret entrance. An entrance she discovered while exploring the castle.

Gwyneth had taken the poison from her mother's cosmetic box. Belladonna was used to redden a woman's cheeks or brighten her eyes. But it was a deadly poison if swallowed.

In the end, Gwyneth's impulsive nature was her worst enemy. She had been spoiled since she was a baby. She was used to getting her way. She did what she wanted, whenever she wanted. Her excitable feelings had finally taken over.

Now, they ruled her completely.

Emmeline sighed deeply. She was free. But Gwyneth might spend her life in a cold, stone cell.

Or in the prison of her own mind.

13

"Emmeline," Father Alban said. His voice called the girl out of her thoughts. "There is something I think you need to see."

He got up and began walking back to the castle.

Emmeline did not want to go back so soon, but she followed anyway. What could the priest want to show her?

They crossed the courtyard and approached the East Tower. She found herself in Pratt's room.

Sir Hugh was there, leaning against the wall. He straightened up when he saw Emmeline. But she had eyes only for the man in the bed.

Richard Pratt was sitting up.

When he saw Emmeline, his face broke into a smile. Not the frightening, twisted smile. There was no longer a hungry look in his eyes. They creased at the corners with real happiness.

His face shone with happiness. White hair floated like a halo around his head.

"My lady!" Pratt said. "Please forgive me for not offering you proper respects. But the doctor tells me I must stay in bed."

"Why—" Emmeline stammered. "What can you mean? I am no lady."

The old man continued as if he hadn't heard her. "And how is your noble father, the chieftain?" he asked.

Emmeline looked back at the priest and young knight. They stood together, speaking in hushed tones.

Her mind reeled with confusion. Something in the back of her mind moved. A rhythm. Like fists beating on a locked door. The door in her memory!

Emmeline began to feel excited. She turned back to the old man with a question.

"What was this chieftain's name?" she asked.

"I was hoping you could tell me," Pratt said. His voice shook as Emmeline's disappointment showed.

He went on. "It was not so many years ago. But my memory is muddled, somehow. I cannot remember," he said.

Sir Hugh spoke. "Probably that knock on the head, eh, Pratt?"

His smile vanished as the old man spoke again.

"Pratt? Who is he?" Pratt asked, scratching his head. "Never heard of him."

"Why, you old—" Hugh said, annoyed. "He's you!"

"Now, young man. Don't go losing your temper," the old man said. "I don't know this Pratt fellow. But my name is the same as it's always been. Michael O'Sullivan."

14

"Do you mind if I join you?" Hugh asked.

"Yes! I mean, no. I—" Emmeline stammered.

Emmeline stopped walking. Over Hugh's shoulder the castle loomed, threatening. Or mocking. She was free now, with a paper to prove it. But now, "free" was just another word for "homeless."

Gwyneth's parents had taken their daughter and left the shire. There was no reason for Emmeline to stay. Or was there?

She looked at the young man before her. For a moment, she allowed herself to dream... but only for a moment. She turned away quickly.

"I must go. I have a long road before me," she said.

With no happy ending.

Emmeline sighed.

"Where are you going, Lady Emmeline?" Hugh's voice held a softly teasing note. "A young woman should not travel alone."

"Still less should she travel with a bold young man!" Emmeline answered.

She fumed silently, stomping down the road. Why must he tease her so? Couldn't he see that her heart was breaking?

She did not look back. She did not see the castle disappear behind the trees. She did not hear the sound of following footsteps.

Which was why she jumped when Hugh's voice said, "So, we're going to Ireland, then?"

"A ridiculous idea. Why would I go there?" she asked.

"Isn't it obvious? Clearly, you were stolen from your cradle. Then brought to England as a hostage. Perhaps to keep your father from starting a rebellion. It's happened to others before you," he said.

Emmeline was doubtful.

"So you really believe Richard Pratt? Oh, excuse me. I suppose we're calling him Michael O'Sullivan now?" she asked.

"Maybe we should believe him, Emmeline," Hugh said. "I've heard what he was like before. But now he's the nicest old man you could wish to see. And you can see right through him, too. Perhaps we'd all be more honest if we had our skulls cracked regularly."

"Well, I don't see how you will manage, Sir Hugh," Emmeline said. "If Irishmen are as hot-tempered as they say. They'll most likely kill an Englishman and ask questions later."

Hugh smiled grimly.

Emmeline kept teasing him. "And I don't see how you plan to solve this new puzzle. All you have is the name of a crazy old man. 'Emmeline' is probably not my real name, either," she said.

"I have made do with less!" Hugh shot back.

Hoofbeats announced the approach of two horses. A rider swung to the ground. It was Andrew, Hugh's squire.

Emmeline's jaw dropped when she looked up. Mary Cooper sat on the other horse.

"Ah! Andrew! Finally," Hugh said. He was cheerful. "I was beginning to wonder about you. So, this is your Mary, is it? Well, I hope she's learned to hold her tongue. I can't stand gossip."

The knight swung easily into his saddle. Before Emmeline could protest, she was dragged up behind him.

Mary giggled from her seat behind Andrew on the other horse.

"Oh, this is so exciting!" she said. "Why, what's the matter, Em? You look positively green."

Emmeline had the feeling her world was about to be turned upside down. Again.

"Hold fast!" Sir Hugh called.

He spurred his mount. Both horses shot away, like twin arrows from a bow. They galloped in the direction of the setting sun.

Epilogue:

Bodiam (modern spelling of Bodyham) Castle is still standing today. It is one of the best surviving castles in England.

Sir John Dalyngrigge was a real person. His father, Sir Edward, built Bodiam Castle around 1390. Sir John probably didn't try to marry a girl who lost her mind. But he did end up getting married to a widow named of Alice Beauchamp.

As I researched for my story, some odd things happened. Real-life facts fit into my fiction in a way that was almost eerie. For example:

There really is a secret passage from a fireplace into the East Tower room. But no one seems to know why it is there.

Some people have heard sounds when passing the castle at night such as revelry (a party), singing, music, and words in a strange language.

Others have seen a lady dressed in red. The ghost stands on one of the towers. She waits in the moonlight, looking off into the distance. But who she was and who she is waiting for, no one knows.

Before I began writing this story, I searched for pictures. I like to have images to look at when writing about the characters.

Later, when I read about the ghosts of Bodiam Castle, I had a funny feeling. Looking back through my file, I found a picture. I had chosen it long before reading about the ghosts of Bodiam.

What did it show? A young woman in a red dress with long, blonde hair. She stands with her back to the viewer, looking out of a castle window. But as for what she sees... who can tell?

About The Author

Hanna Yeager is a contributing author to the Storyshares library.

About The Publisher

Story Shares is a nonprofit focused on supporting the millions of teens and adults who struggle with reading by creating a new shelf in the library specifically for them. The ever-growing collection features content that is compelling and culturally relevant for teens and adults, yet still readable at a range of lower reading levels.

Story Shares generates content by engaging deeply with writers, bringing together a community to create this new kind of book. With more intriguing and approachable stories to choose from, the teens and adults who have fallen behind are improving their skills and beginning to discover the joy of reading. For more information, visit storyshares.org.

Easy to Read. Hard to Put Down.

Printed in the USA
CPSIA information can be obtained
at www.ICGtesting.com
JSHW011940200923
48546JS00008B/87

9 781642 611670